## Dear Parent:
## Your child's love of reading st

Every child learns to read in a different way and at his or her own speed. Some go back and forth between reading levels and read favorite books again and again. Others read through each level in order. You can help your young reader improve and become more confident by encouraging his or her own interests and abilities. From books your child reads with you to the first books he or she reads alone, there are I Can Read Books for every stage of reading:

### SHARED READING
Basic language, word repetition, and whimsical illustrations, ideal for sharing with your emergent reader

### BEGINNING READING
Short sentences, familiar words, and simple concepts for children eager to read on their own

### READING WITH HELP
Engaging stories, longer sentences, and language play for developing readers

### READING ALONE
Complex plots, challenging vocabulary, and high-interest topics for the independent reader

### ADVANCED READING
Short paragraphs, chapters, and exciting themes for the perfect bridge to chapter books -

**I Can Read Books** have introduced children to the joy of reading since 1957. Featuring award-winning authors and illustrators and a fabulous cast of beloved characters, I Can Read Books set the standard for beginning readers.

A lifetime of discovery begins with the magical words **"I Can Read!"**

*Visit www.icanread.com for information*
*on enriching your child's reading experience.*

I Can Read Book® is a trademark of HarperCollins Publishers.

Library of Congress Control Number: 2016952347
ISBN 978-0-06-264071-0

Typography by Brenda E. Angelilli

17 18 19 20 21 SCP 10 9 8 7 6 5 4 3 2 1 ❖ First Edition

# beat bugs™

## Penny Lane

adapted by
Cari Meister
based on a story
written by
Kate Mulvany
Beat Bugs
created by
Josh Wakely

**HARPER**
*An Imprint of HarperCollinsPublishers*

One day Crick sees a penny
rolling into Village Green.
He tries to warn everyone.
No one will listen.
They are busy playing.

The penny comes to a stop
right on top of Crick!

Crick is okay, but he is sad.

He feels like no one

ever listens to him.

Crick wanders the garden.

All of a sudden,

he gets stuck in a web!

Doris the Spider helps Crick out.
It turns out the webs are her artwork.
Doris tells Crick she makes art to
show the world what she has to say.

Crick looks down.

The world does not seem

to care about what he has to say.

He feels invisible.

Doris feels sad for Crick.

She has to do something!

Doris sets a trap.

She catches Jay.

"It's about Crick," she says.

"He needs a little help

from his friends."

Jay finds Kumi, Walter, and Buzz.

He tells them how Crick feels.

"So what are we going to do?"

Jay asks.

Just then, another penny rolls in.

It gives Walter an idea.

They can use the pennies

to build a special place for Crick

so he can be heard and seen.

They just need a name for it.

"I know," says Kumi. "Penny Lane!"

The Beat Bugs get to work.

Even the Army Ants help.

Things do not go so well.

It is a mess.

They need Crick's crane.

Jay goes to find Crick.

"Hey, Crick," Jay says.

"We need you!"

For a second, Crick is happy.

But Jay does not want Crick.

He just wants his crane.

Crick brings his crane over.

"What's going on in there?" he asks.

No one will tell him.

His friends take the crane away.

They leave Crick behind.

He feels left out.

That night Crick is fed up.

He no longer wants to be invisible.

He pushes through the grass.

He climbs up some pennies.

He starts to say something when

the Glowies turn on.

Crick did not know it,

but he had climbed up on a stage!

"What is all this?" he asks.

"It is called Penny Lane," says Kumi.

Crick's friends built it for him!

Crick is happy.

But he does not want

Penny Lane all to himself.

He wants Kumi to use it for dancing.

He wants Walter to use it for acting.

Crick wants all

his friends to share it!

"This space, Penny Lane," he says.

"It should belong to all of us,

so we can all be seen and heard."

That makes everyone happy!

# "PENNY LANE" lyrics
## Written by John Lennon/Paul McCartney

In Penny Lane there is a barber
showing photographs
Of ev'ry head he's had the pleasure
to know,
And all the people that come and
go,
Stop and say hello.

On the corner is a banker with a
motorcar,
The little children laugh at him
behind his back,
And the banker never wears a mac
In the pouring rain,—very strange.

Penny Lane is in my ears and in
my eyes,
There beneath the blue suburban
skies
I sit, and meanwhile back . . .

In Penny Lane there is a fireman
with an hourglass,
And in his pocket is a portrait of
the Queen.
He likes to keep his fire engine clean,
It's a clean machine.

Penny Lane is in my ears and in
my eyes,
There beneath the blue suburban
skies
I sit, and meanwhile back . . .

Behind the shelter in the middle
of a roundabout
The pretty nurse is selling poppies
from a tray,
And though she feels as if she's in
a play,
She is anyway.

In Penny Lane the barber shaves
another customer,
We see the banker sitting waiting
for a trim,
And the fireman rushes in
From the pouring rain,—very
strange.

Penny Lane is in my ears and in
my eyes
There beneath the blue suburban
skies
I sit, and meanwhile back . . .

Penny Lane is in my ears and in
my eyes,
There beneath the blue suburban
skies
I sit, and meanwhile back . . .
Penny Lane.